For Philippa, Richard,
Tim, and Sophie

Copyright © 1993 by Jez Alborough

All rights reserved.

First U.S. edition 1993
First published in Great Britain in 1993 by Walker Books Ltd., London.

First published by Candlewick Press

CANDLEWICK PRESS
2067 MASSACHUSETTS AVENUE
CAMBRIDGE MA 02140

ISBN 0-590-62946-8

12 11 10 9 8 7 6 5 4 3 2 1   5 6 7 8 9/9 0/0

Printed in the U.S.A.   08

First Scholastic printing, December 1995

CUDDLY DUDLEY

Jez Alborough

CANDLEWICK PRESS

CAMBRIDGE, MASSACHUSETTS

Dudley loved to play.
He loved to play
jumping,

diving,

and splashing.
But most of all
Dudley loved to play

all by himself.

The trouble was, Dudley was such a lovely, cuddly penguin

that whenever his brothers and sisters found him on his own,

they just couldn't resist having a huddle and a waddle and a cuddle with him.

"Go away," Dudley would say. "Leave me alone."

"We can't," came the reply. "You're just too cuddly, Dudley."

"I'm fed up with all your huddling and waddling and cuddling," said Dudley one day.

"I'm going to find a place where I can play all by myself." And off he went.

He waddled

and he toddled

for many, many miles

until,
quite by chance,

he found ...

a little wooden house that looked perfect for a penguin.

And it seemed to be empty.

"At last!" said Dudley. "A house of my own – a place where I can jump around all day without being disturbed."

Just then there came a *rap-tap-tap* at the little wooden door.

"It's us," said two of Dudley's sisters. "We followed your waddleprints. Can we come in?"

"No, you certainly can't," said Dudley. "I'm very busy and I don't want to be disturbed, so please go away." And he shut the little wooden door and was alone once more.

"At last!" said Dudley. "A house of my own –

a place where I can splash around all day without being—"

Just then there came a *rap-tap-tap* at the little wooden door.

"It's us," said his brothers and sisters. "We followed your waddleprints. Can we come in and—?"

"No, you certainly can't," said Dudley. "I don't want to huddle and waddle and cuddle. So for the very last time, STOP FOLLOWING ME AROUND!"
He slammed the little wooden door and was alone once more.

"At last!" sighed Dudley.
"A house of my own—"

BANG! BANG! BANG!
went the little wooden
door.

"That does it," he said.
"When I catch those
penguins I'll…"

But it wasn't the penguins at the little wooden door. It was a great big man. "My word!" said the great big man. "What an adorable penguin!"

"Give me a cuddle!" he cried, and chased Dudley all around the house
and out into the snow.

Dudley ran

and ran

and escaped from the man.

Then he decided to head back home. But which way was home?

Crunch, crunch, crunch went Dudley, looking for some waddleprints to follow. But when night came, he was still alone … and completely lost … and now, for the first time, he was lonely. He climbed a hill to get a better view, and at the top he saw

an enormous orange moon with hundreds of tiny sparkling stars huddled all around it.

"Excuse me," said a penguin from the foot of the hill. "Have you finished being alone yet? We wondered, now that you're back … if you wouldn't mind … whether we could … it's just that you're so … *so…*"

"CUDDLY!" shouted Dudley.

And he bounced down the hill as fast as he could.

Then Dudley and all of his brothers and sisters had the best huddling, waddling, cuddling session that they'd *ever* had. Until…